All Ladybird books are available at most bookshops,
supermarkets and newsagents, or can be ordered direct from:

Ladybird Postal Sales
PO Box 133 Paignton TQ3 2YP England
Telephone: (+44) 01803 554761
Fax: (+44) 01803 663394

A catalogue record for this book is available
from the British Library

Published by Ladybird Books Ltd
A subsidiary of the Penguin Group
A Pearson Company
© 1998 Cosgrove Hall Films

Based on The Animal Shelf created by Ivy Wallace

LADYBIRD and the device of a Ladybird are trademarks of
Ladybird Books Ltd Loughborough Leicestershire UK

The Animal Shelf

Little Mut Goes Flying

BASED ON THE ANIMAL SHELF CREATED BY
IVY WALLACE

One afternoon Timothy's Special Animals wanted to build a playground in the garden, but they couldn't agree what to build first. They went on arguing for ages.

Woeful wanted a swing, but all the others wanted a seesaw instead.

In the end Woeful got so cross that he decided to go and build himself a swing in the wood.

The rest of the Animals collected some things for the seesaw – a long piece of wood and an old paint-pot. Then they tried to sort out how they could all sit on it.

Woeful meanwhile had spotted some strands of ivy dangling down from the trees. "This is strong," he said. "Soon I'll have my very own swing. Perfect!"

Back in the garden, Stripey had had an idea. He told Gumpa to find something to stand on. As soon as he was ready, Stripey said, "Gumpa, when I say jump, jump! You're heavier than Little Mut, so when you land, Little Mut will go straight up."

He waited a moment, then said, "Now! One, two, three,

JUMP!"

He was right.
Little Mut did
go up. Up… up…
up… and over their heads.

"Little Mut's flying!" said Getup.

"We must catch up," cried
Stripey. "Come on."

"Well, now we know
our seesaw works,"
announced Gumpa,
and then he
followed the others.

They watched as
Little Mut flew up past
Jick the Jackdaw and up
out of sight.

"Ohohohohoh!" squealed Little Mut, as he fell inside the Hollow Tree. "Now where am I going?"

Little Mut landed safely on the floor of Mrs Mole's cave. The Baby Moles were really pleased to see their unexpected visitor and wanted him to stay. So he had some dinner and then taught them how to play hopscotch.

Little Mut never thought that
his friends would be worried.

But they were. Stripey, Getup and Gumpa were searching everywhere for Little Mut.

"We'll meet at the Shelf when it gets dark," they said.

Gumpa found Woeful on the swing in Bluebell Wood. The monkey only agreed to join the search for Little Mut if Gumpa would give him just one push... then another push... then another push!

Whilst back at the cave, Little Mut and the moles were having a great time too.

Before long, it began to get dark and Stripey and Getup went sadly home.

"Just one more push then we'll look for Little Mut!" said Woeful.

"I'd forgotten all about Little Mut!" said Gumpa angrily. "You're so selfish!" And he gave Woeful an extra hard push.

"Ohohohohoh," cried Woeful, and he catapulted out of sight.

Woeful flew past Squirrel and came to land in the Hollow Tree.

"What are you doing here?" asked Little Mut in surprise.

Woeful thought quickly. "I've come to rescue you. We've been looking everywhere!" he said.

"I'm sorry," said Little Mut.
"We were playing hopscotch."

"Wow! I love hopscotch," said
Woeful and he decided to join in
the fun too.

But the hopscotch continued long after dark, until the Baby Moles fell fast asleep.

"Perhaps it's time to go home," suggested Little Mut. "Thank you for a lovely time, Mrs Mole."

"Yes, come on, Little Mut," ordered Woeful. "Follow my every move."

Soon the two Animals were safely back in Timothy's bedroom. The others were overjoyed to see them.

"Hello, you lot," said Timothy. "I'm sorry I'm late. I had a great time at my friend's house!" Then he continued to talk non-stop about his exciting afternoon. And it was ages before he heard about the equally exciting adventures of Little Mut and Woeful.